LIKE FATHER, LIKE SON

Illustrated by the Disney Storybook Artists

A GOLDEN BOOK • NEW YORK

ISBN: 0-7364-2358-3

www.goldenbooks.com www.randomhouse.com/kids/disney

Printed in the United States of America

10 9 8 7 6 5 4 3 2 1

Bambi's mother can't be with him anymore. His father, the Great Prince, takes Bambi to his new home in the forest.

The Great Prince needs to take care of the herd, so he can't look after Bambi. He asks Friend Owl if he will help find a mother deer to raise Bambi.

Bambi tries to keep up with his dad, but it's hard for a little deer to do.

Finally, Bambi's dad tells him to go off and play with his friends.

Bambi joins his friends at the groundhog show.

Bambi meets a mean deer named Ronno there.

After the show, Bambi thinks he hears his mother calling him, but it is really a hunter playing a trick. Bambi wanders off to find his mother and is almost attacked by some dogs.

The Great Prince shows up just
in time and saves Bambi.

Bambi wants to show his father how brave he can be.

Thumper says he can help Bambi learn how to act brave by looking scary.

Bambi doesn't have much luck when he tries to act braver.

Ronno and Faline are walking through the forest when they hear Bambi. Ronno teases Bambi for not standing up to the dogs.

When Bambi stands up to Ronno,
Ronno chases him.

But Bambi leaps bravely off a cliff, leaving Ronno behind.

The Great Prince is angry with Bambi for being away from home, but he's also proud of his son for making such a big jump.

Trace the line to help Bambi practice his jumps.

While the Great Prince watches Bambi practice, Friend Owl flies in to report on his search for a new mother for Bambi.

Bambi wants to be brave like his father. The Great Prince teaches Bambi to look, listen, and smell for danger.

Bambi watches the Great Prince . . .

. . . and tries to do everything he does.

Bambi keeps getting stronger and braver.

Bambi teaches the Great Prince that there's always time for fun.
How many grasshoppers can you count?

Answer: 14.

As Bambi and his father spend more time together, they grow closer. Use the key to color the fireflies.

COLOR KEY
Red = 1   Blue = 2   Green = 3   Yellow = 4   Orange = 5

Friend Owl has someone he'd like the Great Prince to meet.

Friend Owl thinks that Mena
will be a good mother for Bambi.

Bambi finds out that the Great Prince
has been planning to send him away.

Bambi tells his friends he will miss them.

The Great Prince tells Bambi that he is doing what he thinks is best for his son. He also tells Bambi never to forget that he is also a prince.

Bambi is not very happy when he sees Ronno again. Ronno makes fun of Bambi.

Bambi shows Ronno that he's not going to be pushed around by him anymore.

But Ronno fights back.

When Mena comes to see if Bambi is okay,
Ronno accidentally knocks her to the ground.

When Mena falls, her leg gets caught in a trap.

She tells Bambi to run away because he will be in danger, too.

Bambi thinks of his mother and feels that he can't leave Mena behind.

Bambi gets the dogs to leave Mena
alone and to follow him instead.

The Great Prince hears that there's trouble and comes to help.

Bambi leads the dogs past Thumper and Flower, who try to help him by making brave faces.

When he reaches the mean porcupine's log, Bambi comes up with a plan to use the porcupine to stop the dogs.

It works on one of the dogs!

The rest of the dogs follow Bambi.

Then Bambi remembers what his father told him about listening to the sounds of the forest.

Bambi kicks some rocks down a hill to try to stop the dogs.

The dogs finally give up and turn back.

But more rocks tumble down the hill, carrying Bambi with them.

The Great Prince finds Bambi,
but there's not much he can do to help.

When Bambi runs to meet his father, he falls again.

The Great Prince is very worried about Bambi.
He doesn't think Bambi will be okay.

Finally, Bambi speaks and lets the Great Prince know that he is okay. The Great Prince is very glad.

After a while, Thumper tells everyone how brave Bambi was with the dogs.

Everyone cheers for Bambi,
who now has his antlers.

With some help from the porcupine, the brave Bambi gives Faline a kiss.

When Ronno sees Bambi and Faline together, he warns Bambi that he's not done with him yet.

But Ronno isn't as brave as he makes everyone think he is. When a turtle bites him, he runs away, screaming for his mother.

Bambi leaves his friends to explore
the forest with his father.

They go to the meadow where the Great Prince first met Bambi's mother.

The Great Prince says that he was a lot like Bambi when he and Bambi's mom met.

Now Bambi and the Great Prince will live together in the forest forever.